Maximus
and the
Beanstak

Written by Damian Harvey
Illustrated by David Lopez

Maximus had been busy all day helping his mum and dad. He had fed the goose with delicious golden corn.

He had picked vegetables from the garden.

He had even helped to mend a
hole in the roof of the windmill.
"What a good boy," said Mum.
Dad gave Maximus a shiny
gold penny.

Maximus always kept the gold pennies his dad gave
him for being kind and helpful.

At dinnertime, Maximus put the shiny gold penny next to his bowl. Mum had cooked a huge pile of sprouts. Dad had made a big jug of his delicious fishy sauce.

"Yum!" said Maximus. "Sprouts and fishy sauce – my favourite."

Maximus was about to take a bite when ...

... the cottage began to shake,

the table began to rattle,

the sprouts began to roll off his plate and on to the floor.

"My prize-winning sprouts!" cried Mum.

"My world-famous fishy sauce!" cried Dad.

"My yummy dinner!" cried Maximus.

A huge green beanstalk was shooting up through the floor of their cottage.

It **smashed** through their table.

It **crashed** through their roof.

"Our lovely cottage!" cried Mum and Dad.

"My shiny, gold penny!" cried Maximus.

Dad rushed outside
to look at the roof.
Mum ran to the kitchen
to look for a broom.

Maximus just looked
at the hole in the floor.

He looked, and he stared, and he saw ...

... something climbing up the beanstalk.

He could see tiny little hands.

He could see a tiny little face.

"It's a Tiny!" gasped Maximus.

The Tiny jumped off the beanstalk
and ran across the floor.

"Who are you?" asked Maximus.

"I'm Jack," shouted the Tiny.

"And I spy gold."

The Tiny grabbed Maximus's
shiny, gold penny.

"Hey!" cried Maximus.

"That's mine."

The Tiny stamped on Maximus's hand and ran off.

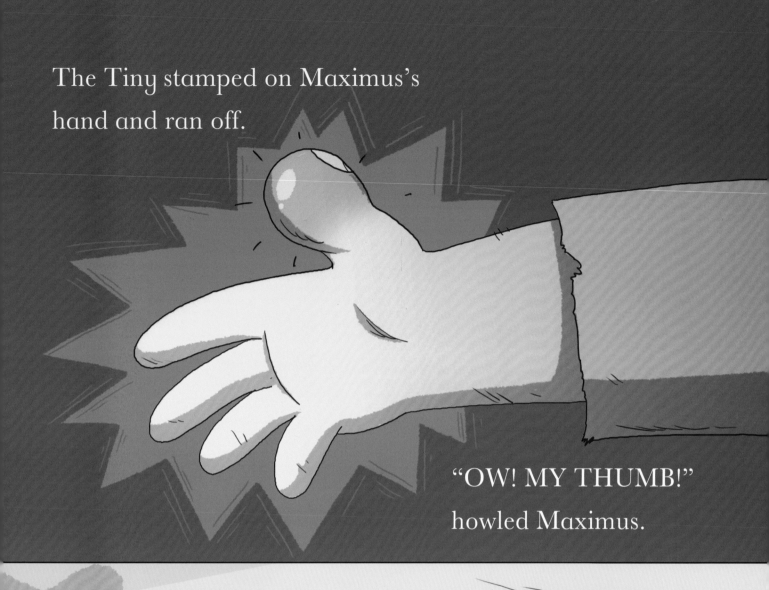

"OW! MY THUMB!" howled Maximus.

The Tiny was nimble and quick and disappeared down the beanstalk before you could say 'Fee, Fi, Fo, Fum', or anything else.

Maximus told his mum and dad all about the Tiny.

"I thought you didn't believe in Tinys any more?" said Mum.

"Tinys are only in stories," said Dad.

That night, Maximus could not get to sleep. He was thinking about the Tiny, and his gold penny. And his thumb was still sore.

So the singing harp sang him songs until he was snoring to his heart's content.

When Maximus woke up, the singing harp was nowhere to be seen.

And someone had spilled his favourite crunchy muesli and broccoli yoghurt all over the floor.

"Who could have done that?" said Dad.

"It must have been the Tiny," laughed Mum.

Maximus followed the trail of yoghurt to the beanstalk.

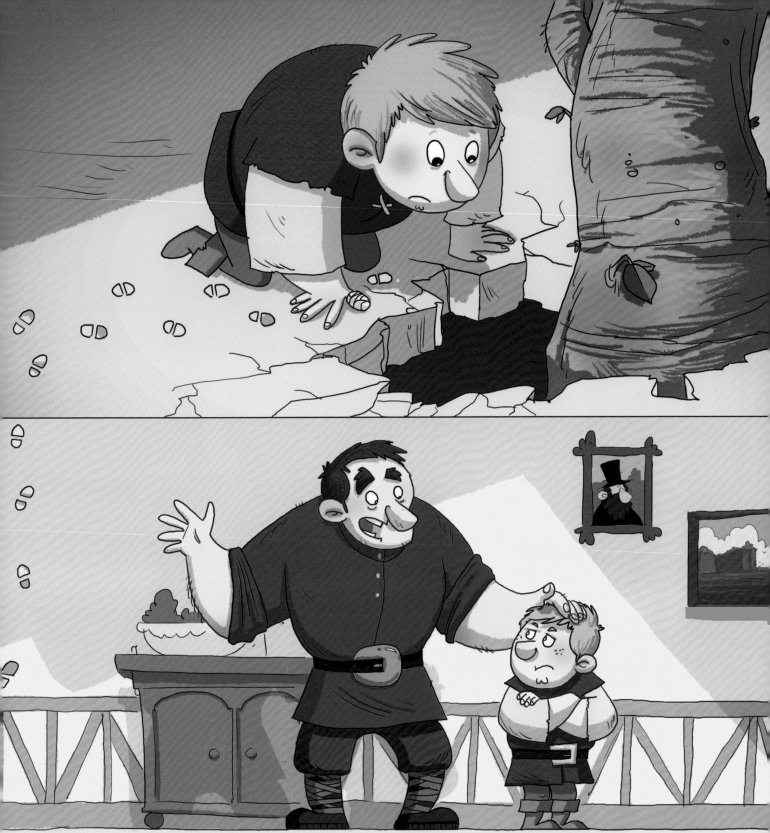

"It *was* the Tiny," said Maximus.

"There are no such things as Tinys," said Dad.

"You'll see," said Maximus.

Later, when Maximus was collecting the goose's eggs,
the Tiny appeared again.

"I spy more gold," said the Tiny.

"I'll give you this golden egg if you give me back my
singing harp," said Maximus. "I know you took it."

"I don't want an egg," cried the Tiny. "I want that goose."

The Tiny kicked Maximus's thumb ...

... and ran off with the goose.

"OH MY SORE THUMB!" howled Maximus, and he ran after the Tiny. He chased the Tiny into the yard where Dad was mending the table.

"Come back with our goose!" cried Dad.

They chased the Tiny into the kitchen where
Mum was baking bread.
"Come back with our goose!" cried Mum.

They chased the Tiny all through the house.

But the Thing was nimble and
quick and disappeared down
the beanstalk before you
could say . . .

'Fee,
Fi,
Fo,
Fum',
or anything else.

This time,
Maximus
followed him.

The Tiny ran into his house and slammed the door. So Maximus knocked on the door as politely as he could.

Maximus told Jack's mum what her son had been up to. He told her about the gold penny, the singing harp and the goose. He told her about the mess he'd made with the muesli and yoghurt. He even told her about his sore thumb. Jack's mum was furious.

The next morning, Maximus ate two big bowls of his favourite crunchy muesli and broccoli yoghurt. Then he ate three pieces of toast covered with his favourite sticky carrot jam.

"Don't worry about the mess," said Jack's mum. "Jack will clean it up."